An American Flag for Their Father

WD Hickey
LTC U.S. ARMY

Ann M. Hickey

Justin Hickey

Meghan Hickey

Annmarie Gifford

www.AHG7.com

An American Flag for Their Father

Annmarie Hickey Georgopolis
Illustrated by Susan Spellman

PUBLISHING WORKS
Exeter, New Hampshire

Illustrations copyright © 2005.
Susan Spellman.

Design by Lauren Hawkins

Published by PublishingWorks
4 Franklin Street
Exeter, NH 03833
(603) 778–9883
www.publishingworks.com

Library of Congress Cataloging-in-Publication Data
Georgopolis, Annmarie Hickey, 1962–
        An American flag for their father / Annmarie Hickey Georgopolis.
        p. cm.
        Summary: As fifth-grader Jonathan and his sister Meghan, a third-grader,
        raise money to buy a big flag to welcome their father home from active
        duty in the Middle East, they get help from unexpected sources.
        ISBN 1-933002-06-9
        [1. Moneymaking projects--Fiction. 2. Brothers and sisters--Fiction.
3. Flags--United States--Fiction. 4. Grandparents--Fiction. 5. Veterans--Fiction.] I. Title.
        PZ7.G29346Am 2005
        [Fic]--dc22

                                        2005047618

Printed in Canada

To Mom & Dad, Thank you for everything.
I'll love you both, always… Re

To my older brother, Lieutenant Colonel Martin Joseph Hickey, who when I first began to write this story, was serving honorably in Operation "Iraqi Freedom" with the 804th Medical Brigade in the Middle East. I emailed the original version of this story overseas to Marty, back in 2003. I wanted to send him a little something to lift his spirits and to remind him of his family and of his home while he was away from all of us for over a year. I'm very happy to say that my brother has since made it home safely to us.

To my father, William Richard Hickey Sr., who served courageously in World War II, storming the beach at Normandy on D-Day and driving a tank under General Patton's command. I'm very sorry to say that my father has since passed away, on July 19, 2004.

I am so very proud of these two fine men. Their selfless dedication to their country and to its freedoms, especially during a time of war, does them both great honor.

I cannot begin to tell you how much I loved my father, and how truly missed he will forever be. But the loss of my father just makes me appreciate and love my one remaining parent all the more, Mrs. Ann M. Hickey of Plum Island. For all of your faithful, loving, generous, intelligent, and kind ways, I thank you Mom.

And finally, but most importantly, to my wonderful husband Jerry, whom I love more than anyone else on this earth; my love, respect, admiration and friendship to you forever, pal.

Acknowledgments

A special thanks goes out to some good friends of mine who took the time to read this story when it was still in its early stages, and they've been so very kind to read other stories I have written in the past, as well. They offered me constructive criticism, editing advice, and encouragement, and I truly appreciate their support and thoughtfulness. Thank you to: my good friend, Carolyn Pompeo; my Aunt Betty (Sister Elizabeth Toohig); Sister Margaret Bickar; Ken and JoAnne DesLauriers; Joan Gerowitz; Mike and Janet Equi and their oldest daughter, Alexandra; Mrs. Kay Sheehan; "The Girls"—Clare Proctor, Marion Jakusiak, Ellie Hooten, and Jeannie Letizia; and for her valuable critiques, DeeDee Hughes. My apologies to anyone I did not mention here by name, who was also of assistance to me. I am full of gratitude to so many kind people. Thank you one and all.

I always felt that if this story ever got published, it would in part be due to my dear old friend, Mildred Letizia. Millie loved to read, and she enjoyed reading some of my earlier stories. I just know that she would have loved this one in particular, about the selling of Popsicles on Plum Island. It was something that we really did do as kids growing up there. Thanks for smiling down on me from heaven, Millie. . . Give Dad my love, and know that you are both missed.

And many, many heartfelt thanks to my wonderfully patient and articulate publisher, Jeremy Townsend, to my talented illustrator, Susan Spellman, to my thorough copy editor, Melissa Hayes and to my creative designer, Lauren Hawkins. Thank you one and all for not only turning my little story into this beautiful children's book, but for also fulfilling a lifelong dream of mine, which is to see one of my many stories professionally published.

"Stop, stop, stop!" Meghan called out, her straight, shoulder-length dark red hair bouncing as she jumped up and down. "Let's get this one, Jon."

Jonathan stopped scrolling through the Web site and looked to where his younger sister was pointing on their computer screen.

"Nah, it needs to be much bigger than that, Meg," Jonathan said, going back to his scrolling. "I mean, we *could* buy that one, but let's see if they have any larger ones. We want to get the biggest one we can afford, right?"

"Yep! The biggest and the best," Meghan concurred.

Meghan watched the blur of American flags as Jonathan continued to scroll. The flags got larger further down the page.

The computer had been a gift from their father, who was a lieutenant colonel in the Army Reserves. He had bought it for them a little over a year ago, when his unit was called to active duty in the Middle East. He wanted his wife, Cindy, and their children to be able to reach him through e-mail every day while he was overseas. He told them it would make his time there go a little faster. Jonathan and Meghan had learned how to use a computer at the Salisbury Elementary School, where Jonathan was in fifth grade, and Meghan was in third. With their mom's help, both children were able to surf the Internet in search of a special homecoming gift for their father.

When Jonathan got to the last couple of images on the Internet site, he stopped scrolling and said, "This is it, Meg. This is the flag that Dad would want flying from the new flagpole in our yard." Jonathan smiled at Meghan, his hair and freckles matching hers. "If we could raise another fifty bucks, that is."

"It's ten feet by nineteen feet," Meghan read over her brother's shoulder.

"Let's really try for that flag, Jon."

Looking on, she said, "Cool! It's humongous!"

Jonathan scrolled up the page, three pictures above their flag. "Well, this is the size of flag that we can afford now with the money we've already saved. But if we earn some more, we might just be able to get that bigger flag for Dad instead."

Meghan replied, "Let's really try for that flag, Jon. I'd love to get it for Dad's homecoming. We need a really big flag to fly from the big flagpole that Uncle Jay built."

"We just need to come up with a way to earn the extra fifty dollars before Dad comes back home in the next month," Jonathan sighed.

"But how?" Meghan asked him, sounding a bit defeated. "It took us all year to make a hundred and fifty dollars. And now that we're out of school for summer vacation, we won't have a chance to collect any more cans or bottles—especially since we're both leaving for summer camp next week."

"Mom said that Nana and Grampy Hickey might have some chores or something we can do while we're visiting them."

Just then their mother came into the room and said, "Okay, kids, are you ready to hit the road? Time to go to your grandparents' house. Remember to take enough stuff for the four days while I'm in Houston. I'll return home sometime on Tuesday; and your grandparents have offered to drop you back off here at our house, late that same day."

The kids nodded as their mom rushed around grabbing last-minute necessities. She was off on a business trip, and the kids were going to Plum Island to stay with their dad's parents. Jonathan and Meghan always looked forward to visiting Nana and Grampy Hickey.

As the kids loaded their suitcases into the car, Meghan looked up at the flagpole. "It sure looks empty without a flag on it. We've just got to earn enough money to buy that really big flag." Jonathan agreed.

"What's up?" their mom asked. They explained about the flag that they wanted to buy for their father and about the extra money they needed to earn. "Well," she said, smiling, "I'm sure you can figure something out. But remember, Dad will love any size flag you give him. You know that, right?" She rushed back into the house for one last check.

Jonathan closed the trunk of the car and opened the passenger door. As he did so, his mom rushed back out. "Okay, hop in!" she said.

"Mom?" Meghan asked. "How many more days till Dad gets home?"

"He said in his last e-mail that the whole unit would be coming home sometime next month. But you know he loves to surprise us, so it could be any time, really."

"But if we're all gone from here, how will he find us?"

"Don't worry, sweetie," Meghan's mom said, stroking her hair lightly, "I always tell Dad where we are. He knows you'll be on Plum Island and that I'll be at my business convention in Houston until Tuesday. I'm sure there will be messages from him waiting for all of us when we return."

"Now," Mom said again, "are you sure you packed enough for four days?"

"Yes, Mom!" Meghan and Jonathan answered at the same time. They looked at each other, giggled and tried to be the first to call out, "Jinx!"

★ ★

It was a quick trip from their home in Salisbury to Plum Island. Their mom
drove along the two-mile road that takes everyone out to the island. As they
passed the Plum Island Airport on their right, Jonathan and Meghan craned
their necks to watch a small plane take off. Past the airport, both sides of the
road were surrounded by marshland and water. As they drove over the Plum
Island Bridge, the kids pointed and cried out as a large flock of Canada geese
flew overhead. Their mom explained that the geese were most likely heading
for the island's wildlife refuge.

Plum Island is really just a large sandbar, nine miles in length, and only a quarter-mile across at its widest point. Seven of the nine miles are made up of the National Wildlife Refuge. Within the refuge, the sand dunes are undisturbed, providing a home to many different kinds of birds and animals. The other two miles that make up the island are where everyone lives. It's a tiny island where a lot of summertime guests and bird-watchers love to visit, and it is where Jonathan's and Meghan's father grew up as a boy. Once over the bridge, it was just one more mile to their grandparents' home on 49th Street.

After unloading the kids and their suitcases, their mother kissed them good-bye, gave each of them a hug, and told them to be good for their grandparents. "I'm sorry to just drop them and run," she told Nana Hickey as she hugged her quickly, "but I'd better get moving if I'm going to catch my plane. Call me when you're bringing them home on Tuesday, just in case I get delayed."

"Don't worry, Cindy. Hurry and catch your plane!"

And with one final wave, she was gone.

"So, children, what would you like to do today?" Grampy Hickey asked after their mother's car had disappeared down the road. "Nana, Grampy, do you have any chores that we could do around your house?" Jonathan asked. "Maybe we could weed your flower garden?"

"Or maybe we could dust the furniture?" Meghan added.

Nana and Grampy Hickey looked at one another, confused. "Chores? But this is your summer vacation—why on earth are you volunteering to do chores?"

"Maybe we could take out the trash?"

"Or wash your car?"

"Or polish your silver?"

"What on earth . . . ?" Grampy's weathered face wrinkled in dismay.

Jonathan explained. "We've been saving up to buy Dad a special gift for his homecoming, but we need to earn some extra money fast. We've been saving

"So far we've saved up a hundred and fifty dollars."

all year long. We put out two large trash cans in the hallway at our school with recycling signs on them so that we could collect all of the used cans and bottles. So far we've saved up a hundred and fifty dollars. It's here in this envelope," Jonathan said, pulling a package from his duffel bag. "We brought it with us to keep it safe until we need it. Can you put it in the bank for us on Monday?"

"Sure," Grampy smiled. "But let's put it in this jar here until then, okay?"

"Okay. But to get what we really want for Dad, we need to earn another fifty dollars."

"And what is this special gift that you want to give your father when he comes home?" Nana Hickey asked.

"An American flag," Jonathan replied.

"We got the idea from you, Grampy," Meghan piped up. "You always fly an American flag here. And Dad always said how much he'd like to have one at our house someday."

"What a great idea!" Nana and Grampy Hickey smiled at the children.

"You see, we've been working on this all year. We told Mom about it, and she chipped in and bought the materials for a flagpole to be built in our front yard. And then Uncle Jay donated his time to build the flagpole for us. Now that it's all built, it's up to us to get Dad just the right flag to fly from his flagpole."

Grampy Hickey said, "But two hundred dollars for a flag—you can't get one that costs less money?"

"Oh, we could. We could buy a smaller one," Jonathan replied. "But Dad would love the bigger flag. And that's why we need to earn another fifty dollars."

"Ahhhh, we see," Nana Hickey replied. "What a lovely thing to do. We're so very proud of you both; and of course, we're very proud of your father as well. It's a very brave thing to be a member of the military. Your dad followed in your Grampy's footsteps in joining the army."

Grampy looked wistfully at the children. "You know, we worry about him, but we are also so proud of him. A nice big American flag for his homecoming would be perfect. That's a wonderful idea."

Nana Hickey volunteered, "You know we'd be happy to give you the remaining fifty dollars that you need, right?"

But Meghan and Jonathan shook their heads. "No thanks, Nana. Dad will like our gift even better if he knows that we earned all of the money, all by ourselves," Meghan said.

"You're right," Grampy agreed. "We're so very, very proud of you."

"Well then, let's see . . ." pondered Nana Hickey. "I know of one job in particular that your father and his brothers and sisters used to do during the summer months, when they were just about your age, Jonathan."

"What's that?" the children asked excitedly.

"He used to sell Popsicles along the Plum Island beach. He and one of his siblings would each hold the handle of an ice cooler, filled with Popsicles. They would walk up and down the beach, asking everyone along the way if they'd like to buy a Popsicle."

"Wow, that sounds like a great idea!" Meghan squealed.

"How do we get started? Do you have an ice cooler we could use? Where do we get the Popsicles?" Jonathan's voice was eager as he peppered them with questions.

"Could we start today?" Meghan asked, looking out at the bright and sunny morning. "It's a great day for the beach!"

Nana and Grampy laughed and put up their hands to hold off the questioning. "I'm sure we still have your father's old cooler downstairs in the cellar. Let me see if I can find it," said Nana Hickey. "While I'm doing that, Grampy can call his old friend, Joe, to see if we can pick up eight or ten boxes of Popsicles from his store, for you to sell. Now you're sure you're serious about doing this? I want you both to understand that it's a lot of work."

"We're positive!" cried Jonathan

"Positively!" echoed Meghan

So off they went. Grampy Hickey called his old friend, Joe, who owned a little convenience store on the island. And Jonathan and Meghan went with their grandmother down into the cellar to find their dad's old cooler. The cooler was there all right, buried under a mountain of old stuff—a pair of old cross-country skis with only one pole, an old basketball that was too deflated to bounce, two pairs of girl's figure skates and many pairs of boy's hockey skates. The children also found an old, worn-out field hockey stick, whose curved head was worn away, several splintered and broken hockey sticks, old baseball gloves whose leather had seen better days, two old surfboards that weighed a ton each, and deflated inner tubes that had been patched summer after summer. Wooden sleds with rusted runners were propped against the wall, along with an old toboggan that looked like it would seat at least five children. There was also a box for each child in the family, labeled with each of their names, which housed

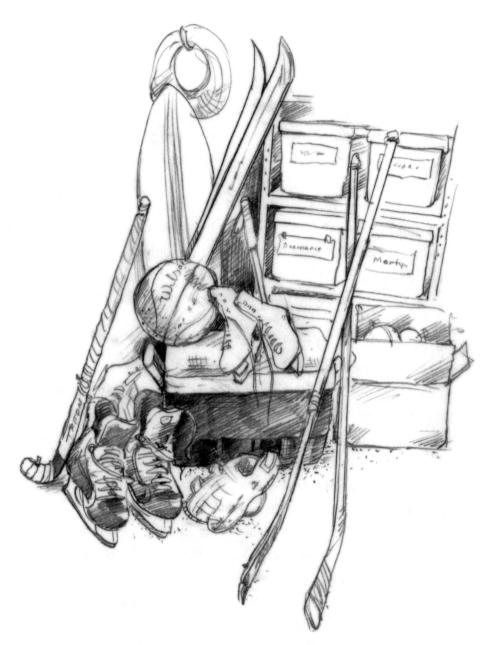

*The cellar held all of their
memories in a large dusty heap.*

all of the trophies, ribbons, and awards that they had won over the years. This had been the home of nine children, and the cellar held all of their memories in a large dusty heap.

Jonathan and Meghan took the cooler out into the backyard. Nana met them outside with some liquid soap and a scrub brush from the kitchen. She turned on the outside hose and helped them clean the cooler, getting rid of all the dust and grime that had accumulated over the years. Jonathan and Meghan washed the cooler again and again, until it was sparkling and ready to go. By the time they were done, their grandfather had joined them out in the backyard. He was grinning from ear to ear.

"Good news!" he cheered. "Joe was thrilled to hear that a new generation of Hickey children would be selling Popsicles on Plum Island beach once again. He said that he'll be more than happy to drop off his remaining eight boxes of Popsicles for Meghan and Jonathan to sell. He'll be down shortly."

While they waited for Joe to arrive, Nana helped Meghan and Jonathan prepare for their day on the beach. "Now, remember—the sand will be very hot under your feet, so you'll both need to wear shoes and socks. And the sun will be very hot, so you'll both need to wear baseball caps and put on plenty of sunscreen." The children lathered the lotion on their faces and arms, and put their hats on their heads.

"Also," Nana continued, "you'll need to stop and drink plenty of water so you don't get dehydrated. Do you have your water bottles filled?" The children nodded.

Nana Hickey gave Jonathan a small fanny pack to wear around his waist. "Jon, you'll carry the water bottles in this. I also want you to take Grampy's cell phone and keep it in your pack. That way, if you get too tired to walk home or need any help, you can call us."

"OK, thanks!" Jonathan took the phone and put it in the fanny pack, along with the water bottles. He felt very grown up and excited about the day now.

Meghan pouted a bit about not getting her own phone, but Jonathan promised her she could use it too.

"There is a zippered center pocket in the fanny pack where you can keep your money. You can charge seventy-five cents per Popsicle, so you'll most likely need to make change for some people." She handed Jonathan ten one-dollar bills and a handful of quarters, dimes, and nickels.

"Finally—and this is the most important thing," Nana said. The children stopped and listened. "Under no circumstances should you accept a ride from anyone other than Grampy and me—okay?"

"Okay," both children responded.

"There," Nana Hickey concluded, "you should be all set."

By the time Joe arrived with the Popsicles, Meghan and Jonathan were ready. They had been practicing their selling technique, repeating over and over with various intonations the phrase, "Do you want to buy a Popsicle? Do *you* want to buy a Popsicle?"

Grampy Hickey introduced his old friend to his two grandchildren. Joe smiled down at Meghan and Jonathan as he shook their hands. "My goodness, I'd know you were Hickey kids just by looking at you. You've both got your dad's dark red hair!" Joe went on to say, "Your grandfather tells me that you want to earn enough money to buy your dad an American flag for his homecoming. Your father will be very proud of you both for wanting to earn the money on your own. Good for you!"

Jonathan and Meghan smiled up at the tall, kindly old man. His words filled them with even more determination than before.

"Well, let's get started, shall we?" Joe suggested.

Joe helped Meghan and Jonathan pack two boxes of Popsicles into the cooler, the maximum number that would fit. Then he showed them how to surround each Popsicle box in the cooler with ice, to keep them frozen. He gave the

*"Your father will be very proud of you both for
wanting to earn the money on your own. Good for you!"*

remaining six boxes to Grampy Hickey to put in his freezer, until the first two boxes had been sold.

Joe showed Jonathan and Meghan how to tear off the cardboard top of each box, inside the cooler, so that they could just reach inside and take out the flavor they needed for each customer. They had chosen a box of orange Popsicles and a box of cherry Popsicles for their first batch. Jonathan and Meghan were now ready to head for the beach and begin selling Popsicles.

"Just have your grandfather give me another call if you aren't able to sell all of these Popsicles while you're here visiting this weekend," said Joe. "You can just pay for the boxes that you sell, okay?"

"Thanks, Joe, but we'll sell them all, you'll see," Jonathan called out confidently.

"You bet," Meghan chimed in.

Joe smiled back at them. "Good luck, kids," he said. He waved to them as he got back in his truck and drove off.

★ ★ ★

Nana and Grampy Hickey's home on 49th Street was just six houses from the beach. Meghan grabbed one handle of the ice cooler and Jonathan took up the other. Nana and Grampy Hickey stood back and watched as Jonathan and Meghan began their walk up the street, the cooler held between them.

"Good luck," Grampy Hickey called. "Sell a lot of Popsicles!"

Nana Hickey called out, "Stop if you get tired. And call if you need us!"

Jonathan and Meghan turned and waved, then walked to the very top of their grandparents' street. Once there, they stood for a moment on the sand dune that looks out over the Atlantic Ocean and Plum Island beach.

"This is so cool!"

"Ready, Meg?" Jonathan asked, as he looked at his sister.

"Ready, Jon!" Meghan replied happily. "This is *so cool!*"

Jonathan laughed. "Here we go!" And off they went down the beach to the left, toward the southern jetties where the Merrimack River meets up with the Atlantic Ocean.

Jonathan and Meghan soon approached their very first customer. She had her beach towel spread out directly opposite 49th Street, close to the water's edge. She was a middle-aged woman who was lying facedown on her stomach, tanning her backside.

"Excuse us," Jonathan asked rather timidly. "Do you want to buy a Popsicle?"

"Oh yes!" She turned over to take a look at the two children standing in front of her, holding their cooler between them. "Thank goodness you showed up. I'm so thirsty, and a Popsicle is just what I need. What flavors do you have?"

Meghan and Jonathan were thrilled. They put their cooler down on the sand near the woman's towel and removed the lid. "We have orange and cherry. Which would you prefer? They cost seventy-five cents each."

"Orange, please, and here's a dollar. Keep the change."

"Thanks!" said Jonathan and Meghan, smiling gratefully. Meghan handed the woman her Popsicle while Jonathan pocketed the dollar bill in the fanny pack. "Have a nice day!" Jonathan called as they moved on down the beach.

At the very next blanket Meghan piped up this time, saying "Hello!" The two of them asked in unison, "Do you want to buy a Popsicle?" Again came a resounding "Yes—thanks!"

They continued to walk up to one person after another, most of whom were lying on their beach towels, asking this same question over and over.

"Sure!"

"I'd love one!"

"Yes, please!" came the replies.

Meghan and Jonathan said "Do you want to buy a Popsicle?" so often that their words began to slur into *WannabuyaPopsicle?* They were amazed at how many people were not only paying for their Popsicles, but were also giving them tips for the door-to-door (or rather, "beach-towel-to-beach-towel") service that Jonathan and Meghan provided.

After an hour of selling, they decided to stop for a drink. Jonathan and Meghan set the cooler down and sat on it, sipping from their water bottles. Jonathan unzipped the center pocket of the pack and looked inside at the money they had collected so far. "Wow!" exclaimed Jonathan. "We've sold lots of Popsicles already!"

He looked up to see how far down the beach they had walked from 49th Street. "Nana Hickey said that from the top of their street to the southern jetties is about a half mile. We're almost there now. And look, we're almost sold out of Popsicles."

"Cool!" Meghan exclaimed. "I'm all rested now, Jon. Let's get going."

By the time they made it to the southern jetties, their two boxes of Popsicles were completely sold out. Meghan and Jonathan took Nana Hickey's advice and stopped once again to drink some water and to rest. They took a seat together on one of the huge rocks that made up the jetties, dangling their feet and enjoying the spray of ocean water on their hot faces. They'd worked hard and were exhausted, but happy.

"Let's take off our shoes and socks, and soak our feet in the ocean, Meg. Then I'll call Grampy Hickey and ask him to bring us two more boxes of Popsicles. We can meet him right over there, on the road to the old Coast Guard Station." Jonathan pointed to the road that was just opposite where they were sitting.

"Cool!" was Meghan's reply. Jonathan shook his head and smiled.

The children walked barefoot into the remains of a wave on the sand. They let the cold Atlantic water run up to their ankles. They chased each wave as it

Resting at the southern jetties.

retreated back towards the ocean and then tried to beat the next one, as each wave curled, crashed, and raced up the sandy beach. After a few minutes, they reluctantly left the water and sat on the rocks again while Jonathan called Grampy Hickey.

"Okay, it's time to go. Grampy Hickey will meet us in ten minutes."

They finished putting their shoes and socks back on, and then hefted the cooler and started walking to the large sand dune where the old Coast Guard Station used to be. While they walked, Jonathan smiled at his little sister. "You're really doing a great job, Meg. I just wanted you to know that. It's awfully hot out here, and the cooler sure can feel heavy at times. Thanks for hanging in there."

Meghan blushed a bit. Jonathan didn't often compliment her, and she couldn't help but be pleased. "I'm glad you're letting me help and not treating me like a little kid. It's been a lot of fun so far. I just hope we can sell enough Popsicles to buy that humongous flag for Dad."

"Me too, Meg." Then he gave his sister a playful nudge and said, "Now let's get going, Squirt. Those Popsicles won't sell themselves."

Grampy Hickey was waiting for them as promised. "Wow, you kids must be quite the salespeople. Two boxes sold out by the time you reached the southern jetties, in just two hours; I'll bet that's a record."

Jonathan and Meghan beamed.

"Nana Hickey wanted me to make sure that you're drinking plenty of water and that you're not overdoing it," said Grampy Hickey.

"We're doing just as she said," replied Jonathan. "We've stopped a couple of times to drink some water, and we took a rest on the jetties before calling you. We're okay, Grampy, honest."

"And we played in the water a bit, too," chirped Meghan.

Jonathan took the two empty cardboard boxes out of the cooler, and Grampy Hickey replaced them with two full boxes. Jonathan and Meghan surrounded the two new boxes with ice, and tore the tops off, just as Joe had demonstrated.

"Your cooler is now repacked and you're ready to go. Good luck! Wherever you end up this time, just call, and we'll come pick you up. Selling four boxes of Popsicles will be plenty for one day, okay? So stop after these are sold out. We don't want you to overdo it on your first day. Besides, you should be taking some time to actually enjoy your summer vacation."

"Oh, we're enjoying ourselves, Grampy," Meghan assured him.

Jonathan and Meghan each took a handle of their cooler and headed back down the road from the old Coast Guard Station to the spot on the beach where they had left off selling Popsicles. They continued walking along the beach, selling Popsicles for another two hours. This time they started at the southern jetties and made their way toward the Point, the northernmost tip of Plum Island. There were fewer sunbathers in this area, and people were much more spread out. Most of Jonathan's and Meghan's customers during this leg of their journey were actually fishermen, out fishing for striped bass in the Merrimack River. By the time Jonathan and Meghan made it to the Point, they had sold their last Popsicle.

Jonathan took out the cell phone once again and this time let Meghan call their grandparents to come pick them up.

"Thank goodness for cell phones and cars," Meghan said, handing the phone back to Jonathan. "I don't think I could have walked one more step."

"You said it. I'm beat," Jonathan said, slumping down next to Meghan on the cooler to wait. In no time at all, it seemed, both kids were back at their grandparents' home on 49th Street. They spilled the day's earnings out on the kitchen counter and began counting.

"Wow! We've already earned twenty dollars, Meg!" Jonathan exclaimed in sheer delight and surprise. "If we can keep selling Popsicles at this rate for the rest of the weekend, we'll be able to get Dad that big flag for sure!"

"You kids did a fantastic job today," Grampy Hickey said as he joined them in the kitchen. "But I don't want you to think that every day will be like today. I'm sorry to say that there is rain predicted for the next couple of days. And few people go to the beach on rainy days."

Jonathan and Meghan looked crestfallen. "Just do the best you can," Grampy said gently. "That's all anyone will ever ask of you. We're very proud of the hard work you both put in today. Now go get washed up and Nana and I will treat you to dinner and a movie out tonight."

With a whoop and a holler Jonathan and Meghan jumped up from the stools at the kitchen counter. They quickly put their day's earnings into the glass jar on the counter, adding to the money they'd brought with them. Then they rushed to get washed and ready for their night out with Nana and Grampy Hickey.

Grampy Hickey's American flag.

Before they left, Grampy Hickey called downstairs to Jonathan and Meghan. "Kids, why don't you come help me for a minute?"

Jonathan and Meghan called back, "Sure, Grampy. Be right there." And they bounded up the stairs to their grandparents' bedroom.

"Since you are going to give your father an American flag as a gift, I thought you might like to help me bring in our flag this evening, before we go out." Grampy Hickey turned and opened the door that led from the bedroom out onto the second-story deck. There, Grampy Hickey's American flag was gently flapping in the summer breeze.

"The American flag means so very much, to so many people. You should always treat it with respect. It represents freedom, and it honors all those people who died in the fight to keep our country together and free. Never let the flag touch the ground. And when a flag starts to tear and becomes tattered, then it should be burned and a new one put up in its place.

"I like to honor the flag by standing for a moment, straight, proud, and tall, as I salute the flag. It's my way of honoring all those good men I served with in the Second World War, and all the other people who fought for our country," Grampy Hickey explained.

"Are they still alive, Grampy, those people you fought alongside?" Meghan asked.

"Some are, Meghan. But many died in the war, and many more have died since, from old age," Grampy said. "There aren't many of us World War Two guys left now."

He continued, "I take the flag from its holder, roll it up, and bring it inside, out of the weather. I do the reverse each morning when I put the flag out for the day. So, would you like to honor the flag with me this evening?"

The children were thrilled. Now they would know what to do when they got their own flag!

"Okay. Come stand on either side of me," Grampy instructed, and the children did as he directed.

"Ready?" Grampy asked.

"Ready!" the children called out.

"Troops, present arms!" Grampy commanded. And he snapped his right hand upwards to the top of his right eyebrow and held it there in a salute. Jonathan and Meghan glanced sideways to see what their grandfather was doing, and then they did the same. They stood there for a moment, standing straight and tall, holding the salute as they faced the American flag.

Grampy then commanded, "Troops, order arms!" And with that, he snapped his hand and arm forward and then back down to his right side, finishing the salute. The children followed suit and did the same.

"Troops, present arms!"

"Excellent," said Grampy. "You two learn fast."

Jonathan and Meghan grinned happily.

Grampy then stepped forward and removed the flag from its holder, being careful not to let the flag droop and touch the deck. He rolled it up and brought it inside into the bedroom. "There," he said. "The flag has been honored and taken care of for another day. If you'd like, you kids can help me put out the flag each morning and bring it in each night this weekend," Grampy offered.

"That would be great, Grampy. Thanks," said Jonathan.

"This is *so cool!*" Meghan added.

And with that, the three of them joined Nana Hickey downstairs, and off they went for their night out.

★ ★ ★ ★ ★

The next morning Meghan and Jonathan slept late. Their grandparents did not wake them. Both kids were tired after walking along the beach for four hours the day before, selling the Popsicles. It had turned out to be a rainy morning just as Grampy Hickey had predicted, so no Popsicles would be sold on this day.

When Jonathan and Meghan did wake up, they were disappointed to see that it was pouring rain outside.

"Maybe tomorrow will be better," Meghan hoped aloud. "Let's turn on the TV and see if we can hear tomorrow's weather."

The children were both disappointed when rain was again forecast for the next day.

"Oh no—this rain is messing up everything for us," said Jonathan.

Meghan said sullenly, "This is *not* cool!"

But Nana Hickey said, "Well, the good news is that you'll both still be with us on Monday. You're not going home until Tuesday. And as of now, they're predicting that Monday will be a beauty of a day. So for the time being, let's have some fun and play cards together. And the two of you can look forward to more Popsicle selling on Monday. Okay?"

"Okay, Nana," said Meghan and Jonathan, hoping for the best.

"Grampy, have you put your flag out yet?" asked Jonathan.

Grampy replied, "Some people put their flag out every day, while others only put it out if the weather is good. I'm in the second group—that way the flag lasts longer. So we won't be putting the flag out today. It sounds like we'll have to wait till Monday for both your Popsicles and my flag."

The rest of the weekend was filled with lots of card games and indoor fun.

"This is not *cool!"*

At last, Monday morning arrived, and the sun was shining. Both kids rushed to get out of bed, get washed, and have breakfast. Before heading out to sell Popsicles, they joined their grandfather in putting out his American flag. They knew now what to do, and no longer needed to be told. Grampy unfurled the flag and put it in its holder. He stood back with his grandchildren and called out, "Troops!" The children stood tall and proud on either side of their grandfather, facing the flag, waiting for their grandfather's next command. "Present arms!" called out their grandfather. And the two children stood proudly and silently beside their grandfather, all three of them saluting the flag together. "Troops, order arms!"

The American flag was flying free—a good start to a beautiful day. Once again, Jonathan and Meghan prepared for another day out in the hot sun by putting on their sneakers and socks, their hats, and lots of sunscreen. Meghan rinsed out their water bottles and refilled them with cold water and ice cubes. Jonathan once again wore the fanny pack around his waist with the cell phone and some small bills and coins for change tucked safely inside. The cooler had been rinsed out and was once again packed with Popsicles. They were ready to go.

Their grandparents kissed each of them on the cheek, wishing them well, as they saw Jonathan and Meghan safely out the back door. Nana Hickey again reminded them to stop and drink plenty of water, to stay together, and to be safe. Grampy Hickey told them to call if they needed them.

Jonathan and Meghan once again made their way to the top of 49th Street. This time, they turned right and headed down the beach, toward the center of Plum Island. They had packed boxes of grape and orange Popsicles for their morning trip. They were ready for their second day of selling.

There were fewer people on the beach today, so it took them three hours of walking a longer distance to finally sell out. They called Grampy Hickey and let him know where to meet them with the next batch.

*They began walking down the beach from where they had left off,
this time with two boxes of banana-flavored Popsicles.*

When Grampy Hickey arrived a short time later, with two fresh boxes of Popsicles, he looked a little worried.

"What's the matter, Grampy?" Jonathan asked.

"Oh, nothing is the matter, Jon. It's just that the last two boxes of Popsicles are both the same flavor."

"So?" asked Jon.

"They are both banana," Grampy explained. "I just don't know how many people will want banana-flavored Popsicles. I don't want you kids to get too disappointed if you can't sell these. Remember what Joe said—he'll take back any that you don't sell."

But Jonathan and Meghan weren't concerned. "We'll do the best we can, Grampy," Jonathan said confidently.

"That's all anyone can ask of us, right?" Meghan added, repeating Grampy's words.

"Right!" Grampy was pleased that the children had remembered his advice.

So once they were packed and rested, Jonathan and Meghan picked up their cooler and began walking down the beach from where they had left off, this time with two boxes of banana-flavored Popsicles.

Jonathan and Meghan soon found that although the grape and cherry-flavored Popsicles had eventually sold out that morning, they were having quite a bit of trouble selling the banana-flavored ones, just as Grampy had predicted.

They started to get a bit discouraged, and wondered if they should keep going or if they should turn around and go home to their grandparents' house. Meghan finally said, "I'm getting tired, Jon. And this cooler isn't getting any lighter."

Jonathan replied, "I know, Meg. I'm getting tired too. And I'm afraid if we're out here much longer, the Popsicles will start melting. I'll tell you what—let's try one more person. If they aren't interested, then we'll call Grampy Hickey and have him come pick us up. All right?"

Meghan nodded, too tired to even speak. And together Jonathan and Meghan trudged up to a kindly-looking elderly woman sitting alone in a beach chair.

"Excuse me, ma'am," Jonathan began. "Would you like to buy a Popsicle?" Jonathan and Meghan asked in unison.

"Well, bless my soul," exclaimed the old woman, and she clapped her hands together joyfully. "I used to *love* Popsicles when I was a girl. I haven't had one in years. What a treat! I don't suppose you have any banana-flavored ones?"

Jonathan and Meghan looked at one another and tried to suppress a giggle. "Yes, ma'am, we do. We have nothing *but* banana-flavored ones. No one else seems to like them," said Jonathan.

"How very lucky for me," the kindly woman rejoiced. "How much do you charge for a Popsicle?"

"They are seventy-five cents each," Meghan replied, as she and Jonathan put the cooler down on the sand. Meghan reached inside to take out one Popsicle for the woman.

The woman handed Jonathan a dollar bill and told him to keep the change.

"Thank you, ma'am," Jonathan said as Meghan handed her the Popsicle.

"Oh no, thank *you*, children. This is just what I needed on a hot day like today." She smiled and asked, "So tell me, children, what toy or game are you earning money to buy?" she asked.

"Oh no, ma'am, nothing like that," said Jonathan seriously. "Our father is overseas in the Army Reserves. He's been gone for over a year now and he's due to come home sometime soon. We want to get him something very special for his homecoming, so we're saving up to buy him an American flag," Jonathan explained.

"And not just any American flag," added Meghan. "We want to get him the biggest one we can. The one we're hoping to get him is ten feet by nineteen feet."

"How many banana-flavored Popsicles do you have left?"

The old woman became very quiet and she looked sad, but then she smiled and said in a voice thick with emotion, "Well, God bless you, children. God bless you. What a lovely thing to do for your father. He's going to be so pleased."

Jonathan and Meghan thanked her.

The old woman asked, "How many banana-flavored Popsicles do you have left?"

"Two entire boxes, minus the one you just bought from us. That's forty-nine Popsicles," Jonathan said downheartedly.

"And you're selling them for seventy-five cents apiece, is that right?" asked the old woman.

"Yes," Meghan piped up. "But no one seems to want them."

"Well, for such a worthy cause and because you've made an old lady so very happy by providing her with her beloved banana-flavored Popsicles, I'll give you fifty dollars for the entire two boxes!"

Jonathan and Meghan just gaped at each other. "Do you mean it? You'll buy all of them from us?" asked Jonathan.

"Cool!" screamed Meghan.

"But wait—they'll all melt before you would ever get a chance to eat them," Jonathan said.

"Oh, bless your heart. You're so honest and considerate. Your parents must be so very proud of you! It's all right. You see, I'm traveling with a busload of friends. And it just so happens that all of my friends love banana-flavored Popsicles too! I know some of us could eat more than one. Oh, here they come now."

Jonathan and Meghan turned in the direction the old woman was pointing and saw a large group of senior citizens climbing off a bus and heading down the beach to where the children were standing. Before her friends arrived, the nice old lady introduced herself as Mary O'Halloran.

Jonathan said, "Nice to meet you, Mrs. O'Halloran. I am Jonathan Hickey, and this is my sister, Meghan Hickey."

As the group walked up to join them, Mrs. O'Halloran first introduced the children to her husband, Jake O'Halloran, and then, as they approached, she introduced each of her friends, one by one. Mrs. O'Halloran told the group about Jonathan's and Meghan's efforts to earn money, and what it was for.

Everyone in the group congratulated the children for their thoughtfulness, but there was a hint of sorrow in their eyes.

Meghan said, "I don't understand. Why do you look so sad?"

Mr. O'Halloran stepped forward and put a hand gently on Meghan's little shoulder and said, "We're not sad, little lady. We're proud. We're proud of your father who is defending this great country of ours. And we're very proud of you and your brother for doing such a good deed."

"So what does your father do in the army?" Mr. O'Halloran asked of Jonathan and Meghan.

"He's a lieutenant colonel with the Army Corps of Engineers. He's over in the Middle East right now, with the 804th Medical Brigade," said Jonathan.

"My Grampy Hickey was in the army too, ages and ages ago, during a big war. He drove a tank in General Patton's army, and he got a bunch of medals for that," Meghan announced proudly.

"He was, was he? And what would your Grampy Hickey's full name be?" Mr. O'Halloran asked.

"Mr. William Richard Hickey Sr. We're staying at his house this weekend, 'cause our mom is in Houston on a business trip, and our dad . . . well, we told you where he is," Meghan answered.

"That wouldn't be Billy Hickey, previously from Lawrence, Massachusetts, would it?" asked Mr. O'Halloran in disbelief.

"Yes!" Jonathan said with surprise. "My grandfather was born and raised in Lawrence, Massachusetts. Why? Do you know him?"

"Do I know him? We were army buddies in that 'big war' that you mentioned. It was World War Two. I just can't believe that I'm standing here talking to his two grandchildren. I haven't seen good old Billy-boy in well over fifty years. And you say he lives right here on Plum Island? Well, I'll be. Would it be too much to ask for you to take us to your grandparents' house?" asked Mr. O'Halloran excitedly.

Meghan looked at Jonathan and shook her head from side to side. Jonathan thought about Mr. O'Halloran's request for a moment and replied, "We can't go with you, but we can give you directions and meet you there."

"Of course; I shouldn't have asked you to go with us. You should never ever accept a ride with strangers, should you? Not even nice ones. But give us directions and our bus driver will take us there."

Jonathan gave detailed directions easily, since Plum Island is so very small. The seniors decided to sit and enjoy their banana Popsicles while the children walked home. "We'll meet you at your grandfather's house in a few minutes, Jonathan and Meghan. But don't tell him we're coming! Let's make it a surprise, okay?"

"Okay! We'll keep an eye out for you, so you'll know where to stop and park your bus," Jonathan answered.

Meghan and Jonathan picked up their empty cooler, pocketed the other forty-nine dollars that Mrs. O'Halloran had given them, and began the walk along the beach, back to 49th Street. Even though they were tired, they found they had renewed energy at the thought of reuniting Grampy Hickey with his old army buddy.

"Boy, won't Grampy be surprised!" said Meghan.

"I can't wait to see his reaction," said Jonathan as they walked swiftly along the beach.

True to their word, Meghan and Jonathan stood at the bottom of 49th Street and kept an eye out for the tour bus. A few minutes later they saw it coming their way. They waved it down and the bus driver pulled over and parked at the bottom of the street.

All of the senior citizens began unloading off of the bus. Mrs. O'Halloran carried a package with her. "Hello there!" Mr. O'Halloran called out. "Jonathan, your directions were perfect. Thank you. Now, where is that grandfather of yours?" he said jovially.

All of the seniors joined Jonathan and Meghan and walked over to Nana and Grampy Hickey's house, a two-story tan house with a lovely flower garden surrounding it. Jonathan knocked on the front door and waited.

"I'm coming," he heard his grandfather call.

Grampy Hickey opened the door and stood there quite surprised to find Jonathan and Meghan surrounded by a large group of people who were all smiling at him. "Jonathan, is everything all right? I didn't think you and Meghan would walk back. I thought you'd call us for a ride when you finished. Who are you?" Grampy Hickey asked the crowd behind his grandchildren.

Grampy's big surprise.

Before Jonathan could speak, Mr. O'Halloran stepped forward with his arms open wide and said, "Hello Billy-boy. How are you, my old friend?"

Grampy Hickey looked at Mr. O'Halloran for several moments and suddenly his face lit up with recognition.

"Jake! Jake O'Halloran! I can't believe it's you, after all these years. What on earth are you doing here? How on earth did you find me? How are you, my old friend?" Grampy Hickey hugged his friend and laughed.

Nana Hickey had come to the front door by then, and she and Grampy Hickey invited everyone into their home. They all sat reminiscing and enjoying one another's company. The children explained how Mrs. O'Halloran had bought all of the banana-flavored Popsicles to share with her friends. Jonathan went on to describe the conversation they had had, which revealed that Mr. O'Halloran knew Grampy Hickey.

Mr. O'Halloran was teary-eyed when Grampy Hickey showed him his World War II medals, proudly framed and hanging on the wall out on the enclosed front porch. "Remember these, Jake? I never thought I'd see them again. But my son Marty, Jonathan's and Meghan's father, wrote to Army Headquarters in Washington, D.C., and requested all of my old medals for me. I was so touched, I can't begin to tell you."

"I noticed you're flying the flag from your flagpole, Billy," Mr. O'Halloran commented. Grampy Hickey nodded. Meghan had walked over to where the two men were talking. She had overheard Mr. O'Halloran's last comment and said, "Grampy puts the American flag out every morning and then he salutes it. And then he salutes it again before taking it in every night. He showed us how to salute the flag, too."

Grampy Hickey and Jake O'Halloran looked at each other and fought back tears. The men had been through so much together during World War II, and the American flag held such deep meaning for them both, that no words were

Grampy's World War II medals.

necessary. Mr. O'Halloran knew exactly what his old friend felt: pride for his country, pride for having done his duty, sadness for all those who had died in battle and a true appreciation for life.

Jonathan sat at the kitchen counter, listening to everything around him. He was busy counting out their Popsicle earnings. He had dumped out and combined the monies that were in the glass jar with their earnings from the fanny pack. He separated out the money they owed Joe for the Popsicles and put that back in the glass jar. He then put the remaining amount into a Ziploc bag that Nana Hickey had given him, returning it to the fanny pack. He called his sister over to him and exclaimed, "Meg, after we pay Joe for the Popsicles, we'll have a total of two hundred and thirty dollars. That means that we made eighty dollars in profits and tips this weekend. We can buy Dad that really big flag now and still have thirty dollars left over! Isn't that amazing?"

"Cool! We're rich!" Meghan exclaimed. And the two of them clapped their hands together and danced around.

Suddenly, there was a knock at the front door. Grampy Hickey and Mr. O'Halloran, who were closest to it, turned to see who was there. Grampy opened the door to find the bus driver. "I'm sorry to be the one to say this, but it's time for us to go," the driver said.

Mr. O'Halloran and the rest of the seniors nodded and started to get up to leave. Mr. O'Halloran turned to the children and said, "Before we go, we have something for you children."

"We can buy Dad that really big flag now."

Jonathan and Meghan looked up, quite surprised at this announcement.

Mrs. O'Halloran handed her husband the package that she had taken with her from the bus. From it, Mr. O'Halloran pulled out a neatly folded extra-large American flag. Mr. O'Halloran turned and said, "Our group just so happens to represent the veterans of this great country. We travel around and visit veterans' halls and replace their old flags with new ones. It is our honor and privilege, therefore, to present you with an American flag for your father."

Jonathan went to reach into the fanny pack on the kitchen counter, to take out their money. "Oh no, Jonathan. This is our gift to you, to Meghan, and especially, to your father. We will not accept money for it, but we thank you for the gesture. You two young people make us old veterans very proud."

Jonathan took the extra-large American flag, folded into the shape of a triangle, from Mr. O'Halloran. He gently caressed the top of it and thought of his father. "Thank you. Thank you, all of you," he said to the entire group.

Mrs. O'Halloran smiled and said, "It's ten feet by nineteen feet—just what you wanted, children."

Meghan blurted out, "This is way cool!" Everyone laughed. She then whispered something to her brother, and he nodded.

Jonathan reached back for the glass jar of money and the fanny pack, both still on the kitchen counter. He handed the glass jar to his grandfather. "Please pay Joe for the Popsicles with this money, Grampy, and please thank him again for helping us this weekend." His grandfather smiled down at him and nodded.

Jonathan then walked over to Mr. O'Halloran and with Meghan by his side, he said, "Sir, my sister and I won't pay for our father's flag, just as you asked. But instead, we would like to donate all of our earnings to your veterans' group. We'd like you to take this money so that you can buy more American flags to give to other kids' dads." Jonathan reached inside the fanny pack and removed the plastic Ziploc bag that contained their earnings. He held it out for Mr. O'Halloran to take.

"Thank you, all of you."

The room went silent.

Mr. O'Halloran looked at his wife and then at his veterans' group. Mr. O'Halloran reached forward and accepted the children's donation. He started to speak, but the words were caught in his throat. He straightened up and nodded to the others.

To Jonathan and Meghan's astonishment, the entire senior citizens' group came to attention, stood tall and proud, and saluted them in unison.

Meghan and Jonathan looked at one another and then at Grampy Hickey and knew what they would do in response.

Together the three of them faced the group of senior citizens in the room. Nana Hickey smiled, while silent, proud tears rolled down her cheeks. Their grandfather looked down at them and asked, "Ready?"

Meghan and Jonathan nodded.

"Troops, present arms!" their grandfather commanded. And Meghan, Jonathan, and Grampy Hickey all snapped a return salute. "Troops, order arms!" commanded Grampy Hickey a few moments later; and everyone in the room finished their salute together.

Just then the doorbell to the back door sounded. "Oh my, this house is busy today," Nana Hickey remarked as she went to go answer it, wiping the tears from her cheeks as she went. A moment later everyone in the room heard her cry out.

There, standing in full dress uniform, was none other than Jonathan's and Meghan's father, Marty. He had returned home to them. They called out, "Dad!" and ran over to hug him tight. Grampy Hickey croaked out a teary, "Marty!" and also joined in the group hug.

"So tell me, what's all this? What have you all been up to this weekend?" Marty asked, seeing the crowd of people in the room.

Jonathan and Meghan quickly explained about selling Popsicles, just as their dad had done when he was their age. They told him how they had earned enough money to buy him the homecoming gift that they had so wanted to give him. Jonathan then showed him the American flag which the veterans' group had just presented to them, and how they had donated their money to the group to buy more flags. Jonathan also told his father how their Uncle Jay had already built them a flagpole in their yard at home, to hang the flag from.

Their father gently took the American flag and held it tight to his chest while hugging his children to him again. "You're such great kids. What a perfect gift for my homecoming. Thank you!" Jonathan and Meghan then introduced their father to their new friends.

Mr. and Mrs. O'Halloran promised to come back for another visit to see Nana and Grampy Hickey real soon. It was time for the senior citizens to leave. The veterans' group walked back to their tour bus, waiting for them at the

"Dad!"

bottom of the street. They climbed on board, and leaned out of the windows when the bus started to pull away. They waved good-bye to Nana and Grampy Hickey, Jonathan and Meghan Hickey, and to the children's father, Lieutenant Colonel Martin Joseph Hickey.

The Hickeys all stood there and waved until the bus was out of sight. Then Marty turned, hugged both of his parents, and thanked them for looking after his children. To his children he said, "Let's get packed up and go home. I can't wait to surprise Mom and get this flag flying on our new flagpole. Ready, troops?"

"Ready!" the children called out in unison. They looked at one another and laughed. "Jinx!"

What a weekend it had been. New friends had been made, old friends had been reunited, and Meghan and Jonathan not only had an American flag for their father, but even better still, they had their father back.

As Meghan so aptly put it, "It doesn't get much cooler than this!"

PHOTO BY RON KAPLAN

Annmarie Hickey Georgopolis was raised on Plum Island, in Newbury, Massachusetts, along with her seven brothers and one sister. At seventeen, she was accepted to both West Point and the US Coast Guard Academy. She chose and attended the US Coast Guard Academy, where she gained a deep respect for those Americans who serve our country. She and her husband Jerry live in East Hampstead, New Hampshire. This is her first book.

Susan Spellman has had the pleasure of illustrating over 25 books with a wide range of topics, from serious anatomical studies for science books, to a more whimsical style for children's books, and for the children's magazine, *Highlights*.

In addition to commercial art, Susan pursues an interest in fine art and has exhibited in galleries and art associations. She lives in Newburyport, Massachusetts, with her husband and daughters, and frequently enjoys spending time on Plum Island, the setting of this story!